CHLOE

VISIONS OF THE FUTURE
A BLOOD PROPHECY NOVELLA

BARB JONES

World Castle Publishing, LLC
Pensacola, Florida
Copyright © Barb Jones 2016
Paperback ISBN: 9781629894911
eBook ISBN: 9781629894928
First Edition World Castle Publishing, LLC, July 18, 2016
http://www.worldcastlepublishing.com

Licensing Notes

Cover and Art Design: Steven J. Catizone
Editor: Maxine Bringenberg

ACKNOWLEDGMENTS AND DEDICATION

This book is written for the Blood Prophecy Street Team—The Queen's Champions: Amy Bernal, Barbara Burdette, Dee Knope, Jodi Wilkins, LeAnn Franz, JoAnn Boothby, Arianna Jones.

This book is also dedicated to a special friend Frank, who is a character in this short story, as well as to my children—Arianna and Kaiden Jones. I write for the pure passion, but these novellas are really meant for my fans to tide them over between each novel.

Thank you also to all the readers and fans of Blood Prophecy! You are what makes this series great!

CHAPTER ONE
VISIONS

On a hot June Friday night in 2003, Chloe suddenly woke up and looked at the clock. It read 12:15 a.m. and her house was completely asleep. She knew her mother was in bed, and Tom was in Yakima at the coven. Two months of summer vacation before starting high school. Ugh. Her first year as a freshman. This was NOT going to be fun. Tom and her mother had decided that she needed to go to a Catholic high school and Seattle was just full of them. But there was one in particular that they wanted her to attend. Maybe it was because one of the teachers was her mother's friend and knew about them. Still, it was not going to be fun. But first to enjoy the summer!

Thinking about going to a school with interesting classes, no more uniforms, and boys made Chloe giddy inside. Perhaps too giddy, because she couldn't go back to sleep. Her mind kept racing. She'd chosen Algebra 2, Biology, Ancient Civilizations, Ancient Religions, British Literature, and Latin as her main classes. She was curious about the other kids in the school, and tomorrow she was going to see some of them.

Chloe tossed and turned some more before she started thinking about her history as a witch. Would the others let her fit in with them or think she was too strange? Ever since she could remember she'd had the sight, the strongest powers in her coven, and a unique ability to see into people's pasts by touching artifacts or objects.

She decided that it was time to get up. Chloe managed to climb out of bed and threw on a rumpled shirt and pair of shorts that were lying on the floor. She looked in the mirror at her disheveled hair and whispered a phrase. Instantly her hair was straight and even.

She stared at her reflection and thought, *It's so cool to be a witch*. The first time she realized her potential was the day when she announced to Tom that the whitefish would be killed by the sky. Chloe recalled the puzzled look on her mother's face, yet when the whitefish were killed, a power inside Chloe had awakened. She never spoke of it because she knew it made her different, more powerful than any other witch in the coven. So many events happened that triggered her power, but she didn't speak of the power that grew inside her. In her mind, she could sense a strong growth in her, but it was unbridled, uncontrolled. This power made her warm inside and confident.

Another event that she remembered was that in school, she would touch objects that belonged to others and was able to tell about that person's past. One little girl in class was always alone, and she missed school some days but was never sick. Chloe touched her sweater one time and saw an image that made her upset. The girl was getting beaten by her father, and Chloe told the teacher. Even though she saved the other girl, the kids in the class called her horrible names. Eventually it was so uncomfortable that her mother and Tom agreed that they should move away from Yakima.

Chloe hid the pain from those she loved each day. A strong face and a fake smile was what she showed the world, her mother, and Tom. They didn't think anything was hurting her. Chloe stopped reminiscing as a tear flowed down her cheek. She wiped it away and gave a strong look in the mirror. She was not going to let anyone see her pain.

She came barreling down the stairs in a frenzy and disturbed Marlene, who was sleeping on the couch. A glass of wine sat on the coffee table next to a picture of Tom. "Chloe, slow down. You should be sleeping. What's wrong?"

Chloe didn't stop to answer her mother. "I felt like something called me out of bed. Too weird," she said as she yawned and rubbed her eyes. Chloe loved her sleep and did not like to be woken up for any reason. Nothing in the world could've dragged her out of bed, except for this.

As Chloe sat down to talk to her mom, the phone rang. Marlene did not answer it because she had made a promise to Chloe that was always kept, and Chloe knew it. Nothing would interrupt them if Chloe needed to talk. This promise had been made when they moved to Seattle.

Chloe moved a strand of hair from her face

and pouted. Taking a deep breath, she thought about telling her mom about her dream. Her shoulders came down as she exhaled.

"Okay, here goes my new level of insanity. I dreamt that I saw me, but I was older. I looked really hot. There was this redhead girl with me, but I couldn't see her face. She had fangs and all. She was a vampire, but we were laughing. But then, out of nowhere came this man with a dark hat and trench coat. He had a sword strapped to his back. But, then I saw another man. He was really cute, but he kissed me before he bit into the neck of another man. Ewww, what the heck? Me kissing a vampire? The next thing I knew, we were all trapped in flames. And then I woke up."

***

Marlene looked at Chloe and noticed the fear on her daughter's face. More than anything, she had spent the last nine years protecting her daughter from a strange world that existed, but not everyone was aware of it. Chloe was taught about the other races — the vampires, the werewolves, angels, demons, you name it — but nothing had prepared her for the premonitions. That was the one thing that couldn't be taught to Chloe. Tom and Marlene had known this day would come when they read the cards for Chloe's future. Every powerful witch, gypsy, fortuneteller, etc., that they saw all said the same thing. "Chloe is the most powerful witch in the world. As her teachers, you will need to teach her everything, and don't let her education stop. The stars have been aligned since her birth. She will bring the past into the present and into the future of the world. Her destiny has been set." Words that scared both Marlene and Tom.

All Marlene could do at this moment was hold her daughter, comfort her, and listen. Guiding Chloe had always been a challenge, because she was such a headstrong and independent young woman. She even recalled how Tom loved teaching her years ago and the way he loved Chloe then and now. Every stubborn piece of her daughter.

While holding Chloe, Marlene heard the words in her mind once more. *Her destiny has been set.* For years she'd tried to put this out of her mind so she wouldn't think about what Chloe might become. She knew about the prophecy, the tales of the witches' fate depending upon it, and the mere thought sent chills down her spine. Marlene held her daughter closer so not to cause her worry.

12

"Chloe, dear, it's okay. Listen to your dreams. The dreams are telling you something. The 'older you' that you saw...what was she doing in your dreams? There is a clue somewhere, honey. Think slowly back to your dream."

"Okay, Mom. Let's see. I had my hands outward, even with the vampire kissing me. Light burst from my fingertips and shot into the man with the trench coat, but it didn't kill him. I've never had light come from my fingers. Is that a new gift? It does look cool. The redhead — she's pretty, I think. But there's something around her. A strange aura. And there's another man. He's cute but very feral like. It's like he's an animal or something. But, then I changed. I wasn't me anymore. I became a white hawk and then a silver dog, I think. It's not a dream but a nightmare. Can we please go back home to the coven? Please, Mom. I can't stand these dreams, and they started only a few weeks ago."

Marlene held Chloe closer, putting her fingers through her long hair, soothing her. It was such a tender moment until the phone rang again, and a voice in Marlene's head spoke loudly to her. Marlene knew Tom's voice, especially when he spoke to her in her mind. Marlene, a stubborn woman, didn't pick up the phone right away. Again, Tom's voice bellowed in her mind, only this time it was louder, much louder. DON'T ANSWER THE PHONE, MARLENE! USE YOUR POWER AND RUN!

Trembling, she moved away from Chloe so that the poor dear wouldn't see the look of dread on her face. Marlene reached for the phone and gently picked up the receiver. "Hello." There was no voice on the other end for a few seconds. All that she heard was a strange hissing and then a chant...a chant that she had heard only once before, a very long time ago. But it couldn't be him. It couldn't be that vampire that the coven told stories about. He was supposed to be senile. Or was it just a myth? Vampires were known to create myths about their existence to hide the truth. There was a longstanding hatred between vampires and witches, just like there was between vampires and werewolves, but in the end, the vampires hated the witches only because of their craft and connection to a fabled prophecy. But this chant was old and powerful, and known to affect only the strongest of witches.

She turned to Chloe and noticed that the

whites of her eyes had become a strange silvery blue color, and then she fainted. Dropping the phone, Marlene ran to her daughter and tried to revive her.

"Chloe, Chloe. Wake up! Wake up, baby girl."

There was no response from Chloe. Marlene ran to the phone and hung it up. Picking it up once more, she called Tom. She couldn't call 911 and tell them, "My daughter fainted because of a chant." That would surely get some strange reactions. Tom didn't answer his phone, so she tried to call him again. This time he answered.

"Hello, this is Tom."

"Tom, Marlene. Something's happening to Chloe. A chanting came on the phone when it rang and now she fainted. Her eyes are different. You need to come."

"Slow down, Marlene. I'm already on my way. I sensed something with Chloe and decided I needed to be there now. I should be there in two hours tops, but get her into bed. I knew you two should never have left the coven. It is safer here. She is a strong witch! It will be all right. I sensed the old vampire and that's why I communicated telepathically to you." Then he hung up.

Marlene's hands were sweating. After all her years as a witch and studying, this was certainly not something she was prepared for. How strong was her daughter? Was she the one that the Witch's Prophecy kept talking about? She couldn't be. But first things first. She used her power to carry Chloe back upstairs and tucked her into bed. The magic came in handy at times, but she tried not to overdo it because magic took a lot out of her. Then, all she could do was wait. Two hours seemed to drag on for a lifetime. Or at least it felt that way.

CHAPTER TWO
GIFTS

Tom spent the next two hours driving frantically from Yakima to Seattle. Well, actually Burien. Marlene and Tom had decided Burien was a good suburb in which to raise Chloe and try to give her a normal childhood, a life that included the humans and the witches. A perfect balance. Tom loved her as his own little girl, but though he was very fond of her, he was also a little jealous that Marlene only had eyes for her. But, he was a patient man. He and Marlene had their dates, their intimacy, but deep down, he wanted them to become part of his family. Tom loved Marlene and Chloe. After all, he had helped raise that special girl.

Throughout the drive, Tom listened to the various music that played from his radio.

Tuning it all out, he thought of Marlene. Her beauty rivaled that of any other woman he had seen. She had a dimple on the left corner of her mouth, and her eyes always seemed to hold a secret, but it was a secret that they kept between each other. He knew she loved him and he loved her. There had to be a way to make it permanent. But now, Chloe's state wiped that loving thought from his mind. Tom had to get there. Pushing down harder on the pedal, the Corvette raced faster towards its destination.

Tom called Marlene, and she picked up immediately. "There has been no change in her. Tom, I'm so scared. I know she's supposed to be this powerful witch for us all, but she's my only baby. How close are you?"

Tom looked at the side of the interstate. His face began to grimace. Only ninety miles to go. "Sweetheart, I'll be there in under two hours. Hang on."

"Her pulse is steady, her eyes are closed. Breathing normal. She's alive but she's not moving. I can't lose her, Tom. I can't lose my baby."

"I know, sweetheart. But in order for me to get there, I can't talk on the phone because I'm going to do things that I don't need distractions for. Also, the coven leader gave me some additional herbs for you and Chloe. We'll talk as soon as we get there. And listen, I don't have to be back anytime soon. I'm here to stay as long as you and Chloe will have me." Without waiting for a response, Tom clicked the phone off and his foot pressed harder on the gas pedal.

The Corvette revved up and the tires started to squeal. He was literally taking the corners of I-90 at ninety-five miles per hour. This was an insane way to drive, but when Tom had told the coven leader about Chloe, she explained that this was a physical and magical change related to her sight. But Marlene was not prepared to teach Chloe the sight and its full potential. That was Tom's job to do. So he had to get there, and FAST.

***

Chloe was fully aware that her mother had not left her side. Her mind was racing as she heard the conversation that her mother had with Tom. She couldn't open her eyes nor speak, but in her mind's eye—that's what they call the sight—she could sense that powers were awakening within her. Concentrating, Chloe called on her power within.

Relaxing her thoughts, she began to feel at

peace. A powerful voice came from deep within her mind. *Child of the Prophecy, relax. Breath. Relax. Channel your inner voice. Listen to that voice. Your powers are not at their full potential. Receive the power of premonition and be warned. Child, there is one who will come for you. He will take what he wishes and leave you with something. Do not struggle, for the powers mean for it to be. I am your spirit guide. Heed my words. Let this come to be.*

Chloe finally was relaxed enough that her body began to awaken. Her right hand reached up in search of Marlene. Eyes opening, a soft voice emerged from her.

"Mom, I'm all right. I have received another gift from the powers that be. Let me explain."

CHAPTER THREE
FUTURE

Tom didn't knock on the front door. He ran through the house and right to Chloe's room. He knew Marlene well enough to know that she would have put Chloe in her room to rest, as any strong mother would. Hugging her, he realized that this woman was his love. His soulmate. He knew that there were more important things to think about now, but as soon as he could, he would profess his love for Marlene and seek her daughter's blessing.

Chloe lay there on the bed, peaceful as could be. Her breathing seemed steady and Tom rushed to her side.

"Marlene, has she said anything to you?"

"Only that she received another gift, and that she now carries the gift of premonition. If

21

she doesn't honor the gift, it will be taken away. I don't understand."

"Okay, let me look at our girl."

Laying a hand on her forehead, he opened himself to her. He searched her consciousness for any sign from the powers that be. In his mind, he saw images and couldn't quite make them out, so he remained quiet. The last thing he wanted to do was disturb the visions, as he was a guest in her conscience. Images raced through her mind in fragments. Tom saw pictures of a vampire with an older version of Chloe, a redheaded woman laughing with Chloe, and images of wolves. Chloe remained still.

"It's true. Our girl not only has the gift of sight given long ago, but the gift of premonition. She must be taught immediately. No child of our coven has received such a gift at a young age. This is a true sign. The Witch's Prophecy is unfolding. We knew she was the one. This is just further proof."

Tom smiled at his little witch. As much as she had an independent streak in her, she was still a little girl with strong powers. If she ever fell into the wrong hands, the Witch's Prophecy might not come true. The coven of witches all counted on this one child. He realized how sensitive this training must be for her, and he left the room to make a phone call.

***

When Chloe finally regained enough strength to stand on her own, she suddenly had a sharp pain in her head that caused her hand to cover her forehead as she screamed. Pain ripped through her as pictures filled her mind. Pictures of a man with dark hair and a woman with red hair pulled back in a ponytail. She was running, but Chloe couldn't make out from whom. Her vision played out in more detail.

The woman had a charm necklace and was running up the street. The buildings looked like it was in a large city. She slammed her hand on her wrist to stop the watch, gasped for air, once, twice, three times. She bent over with her hands on her knees. She stood straight up again and wiped the sweat from her forehead. A man behind her was also gasping for air, but wanted to catch the red haired woman. She hammered on, breathing hard, but still running well. The man was after her.

Then the vision stopped.

"Mom, I'm okay. Really. Stop fussing. I think I just need some air."

"Okay, honey," was all Marlene could muster out loud. Chloe was gifted with the sight, and it was becoming obvious that she had a connection to the prophecy. The details of the prophecy had not been clear when Chloe learned the prophecy as a small child, and they were still not clear now. All Chloe knew was that she was chosen for a special purpose involving witches, the undead ones as she called it, and God only knew what else.

Chloe went out to the porch and really started thinking about her vision flashes. The night air felt cool against her skin. She loved the Seattle weather. It was definitely different than Yakima. She had never experienced anything like this. As she sat in the wicker rocker chair, she leaned back and closed her eyes. In her mind, she began to remember the vision. The man stood out the most, but she had never seen him before. He had dark hair and mysterious eyes. He was definitely older than Chloe, and he was really handsome. Chloe giggled at the mere thought of that. But, there was something strange about the man. He was in a running suit but there was something weird about him. Chloe had learned about auras from Tom, and this man's aura was not like anything she had seen before. There were no colors around him, just animals. Well, one animal—a dog or something…maybe a wolf. Chloe then focused her mind on the woman. She was definitely beautiful, with red hair and a strange marking. She, too, had the most unusual aura. Chloe then cleared her mind and began to focus on other things.

***

Tom called the coven leader, and they spoke at length about the gift. Unfortunately, he didn't like what he heard. There had been an attack on the coven by one of the undead, and all that the witches understood was that he was after Chloe. What the hell? He listened as the leader said that fourteen witches were found drained of blood.

"Tom, listen to me. Listen carefully. No one divulged Chloe's whereabouts, but you know vampires. They can compel you, and unfortunately, Sister Clara was such a victim. She managed to tell him that Chloe and her mother are in the outskirts of Seattle…Burien, in fact. I know the child can see premonitions now. Can you get them to safety before he arrives? He could be there at any moment. Hurry!"

"Look, I'll do what I can. But I won't be able to return. Not yet. I need to stay with them. Blessed be."

Tom hung up the phone and, shoulders feeling heavy, he went to find Marlene. They needed to get out of there, and FAST!

CHAPTER FOUR
CHAOS

The vampire sat in his car, driving at a speed that seemed impossible on I-90 to Seattle. Normally the traffic was thin at this hour of the night, but he had every intention to get to this witch girl quickly. Having breached the coven, he knew their weakness. Chloe was her name. He needed to connect with her before it was too late. His black Mustang sped along each and every curve of the freeway, and he bypassed the truckers like it was a race. He glanced in the mirror and saw that no one was behind him. I-90 was known for curves at times due to mountain passes, but for the most part, it was straight from Yakima to Seattle.

At the same time he did, a front-wheel drive vehicle came around one of the curves slowly, with two men in the front seat. The tires squealed some as they sped around the curve. As the car came closer to the Mustang, the vampire put his hand on his chin and stroked it as he carefully examined the car behind him in the mirror. He recognized the council members...it was Gerard, that greedy, fat bastard, following him again. *Why can't he just leave me alone? We have no business together right now. Damn,* thought the vampire. He needed to help move the prophecy along. It was taking forever for things to happen.

Kabos was the vampire's name. With his dark hair and dark eyes, he had a certain European look to him. He'd been a vampire for a long time, and he recognized the feelings that drew him to the witch girl. The powers of the prophecy had played havoc on his life, but all these years he had groomed Michael in preparation. Now he needed to just nudge the witch and see if she was the one. After all, the coming queen was going to need a friend and a witch. Kabos sighed and began to sing a song.

Kabos continued driving. The car behind him slowly caught up with him, then paused. The driver stopped in the middle of I-90, selected the reverse gear, and turned around to go in the opposite direction of traffic. Kabos breathed a sigh of relief, because the last thing he wanted was to deal with the council members. He slowly moved into the city limits of Seattle to find a place to sleep. Dawn was approaching.

***

"Chloe! Marlene! Get your bags packed now! We need to leave. Only take what you need for a few weeks. Trouble's found you, and we need to get someplace else. Chloe? Marlene? Where the hell are you?"

The house was silent and Tom got an uneasy feeling. As he moved through the house, Tom started to sense another presence, but it wasn't a witch. The stench was undeniable. How was this shit possible? *Damn prophecy*, thought Tom. His fingers were prepared to unleash his power if anything happened to Marlene or Chloe.

Moving silently though the rooms, he came to Marlene's bedroom. There was no stench, but the smell of blood was strong, and fresh. His only thought was of Marlene as he approached. What he saw next terrified him. Marlene was held against the wall by an invisible force. She was alive…her mouth hung open as if she were screaming, but no sound came out. He couldn't believe it. What in the fucking world could do this to a witch?

29

Tom touched her face with his right hand. Marlene's head turned towards him and her eyes became a dark color. Closing his eyes, he reached into her mind, hoping to get the last images, but a voice erupted from her, causing him to lose his focus.

"Foolish warlock. Do you not understand the powers that be? You tempted fate by teaching the child. You were never to prepare her for the prophecy. Through her comes the fate of another. My beloved Sarah will one day rise and fulfill the prophecy, not this child. Her fate is sealed to the cold ones. Heed my warning now, the Witch's Prophecy will not survive. The child will die before her power becomes too strong."

Marlene's body crumpled to the floor and she lay unconscious but breathing. Tom started to cry in deep heaving sobs. He carried his true love to her bed and let her sleep, then cast a protection spell on her. He knew she would awake when the time was right. He had recognized the voice however; it was the Dark Man. The man that tormented the witches, but had been the so called lover of Sarah Good. Or at least that was what the tales said.

Tom's thoughts turned to Chloe. *Where the*

hell is that child? He had to find her before there was any more trouble.

BARB JONES

CHAPTER FIVE
TRUTH

Chloe, feeling better, decided to go back to bed. Given the late hour, she fell fast asleep. Somewhere between sleep and awake, her visions overpowered her, but in the sleep mode, it wasn't painful and she slept right through it. Images of vampires, witches, and more swirled through her mind. Chloe tossed and turned enough to get tangled in the sheets. In her sleep, she called out, *"In oră vine regina. Ea va fi o."* (*Translation: In the hour comes the queen. She is the one.*)

Abruptly woken by Tom, Chloe was frantic. She listened as he told her of her mother and the voice that spoke through her. All her life she had been told tales of the Dark Man, but this was unbelievable. The Dark Man had come for

33

her mother and her.

"Chloe, pack a bag. Now. There is no time to be upset. We can do that later. Somehow not only is there the Dark Man, but a vampire is coming for you. We have to go. We need to leave your mother here."

Chloe rushed about the room, throwing things into a duffle bag. She always had an emergency bag packed, but this time, two changes of clothes were not enough, especially if there was no chance of coming back. She held onto Tom for a few minutes, enough to let a good cry out before they had to leave. She loved Tom and trusted him, no matter how confusing this must be.

They spent the night in a five-star hotel in Seattle. She'd seen pictures of the Four Seasons Hotel but never had the chance to stay there. She asked Tom why he chose this hotel.

"Chloe, it makes sense. Vampires or others will not think to look for you here. They are going to think I took you someplace else. I'm going to cast a cloaking spell on you, a spell to make you hidden to the world. Only those connected to the prophecy will sense you, but the key is their connection. If they work against the prophecy, they won't see you. Understood?"

Chloe nodded. She got the idea, and all she cared about was bed. She was exhausted and about ready to collapse. While she slept, she dreamt of her mother. Tears of blood trickled down her cheeks, but she never woke. In her mind's eye, images plagued her thoughts. Images of a hunter, vampires, werewolves, and the red headed woman…again. But in her heart she knew her mother was all right. Their bond told her that.

***

Chloe woke the next morning with a slight headache, but she recalled the visions and the events. Knowing that her life was now in turmoil and what Tom had endured, she decided to let him sleep. Quietly, she got dressed and decided to explore the hotel. As she wandered around, she began thinking of her favorite phrase, "My spidey senses are acting up again." This feeling was what made her always feel different than the other kids, but it was an important feeling. It usually told her if something was off. And it was.

She looked around the hotel lobby and didn't see anything unusual. She made her way to a payphone near the elevators. Picking up the receiver, she tried not to think about the germs that were on the phone. She missed her BFF Kathy. Kathy always knew how to make her feel better. Her hands twirled the cord of the phone as she listened and counted the rings.

One ring, two rings, three rings...finally someone picked up. It was Kathy.

"Hello."

"Hey Kathy. It's me, Chloe. Do you think I could come over? I'm, uh, going through some stuff and need to talk. Please."

Kathy and Chloe had been best friends since the day she moved into the new neighborhood. Chloe knew that Kathy wouldn't let her down, especially since Chloe kept her secret about kissing any boy that would give her a dollar. Wow! Kissing sure was expensive.

"Sure, Chloe. Come on over, bestie. I'll have Mom make us pancakes!" Then there was a click.

Ever since she'd seen the whitefish get swallowed by the sky, Chloe had known she was special. Chloe was a strong and powerful witch, and she progressed in her studies with excellence and prowess. She could pick up objects with her hands and tell things about them that no one else would know. She had a gift. Chloe also knew about the prophecy, but no one had ever said anything to her about the gift of premonition. And now, her mother was in a deep sleep and couldn't help her. Or at least that was the impression she got from Tom's explanation.

In the lobby, another attack came. Bending over, her right hand clutched at her waist, she closed her eyes and opened her mind to what she saw. Never practicing premonitions before, she just instinctively knew what to do, but the pain was excruciating. With another part of her power, she reached out through the hotel, searching for Tom. He was still sleeping.

Inside she was laughing. No one — not even her mother — knew the extent of her power. Chloe even amazed herself at times. Silently, she spoke to Tom.

Tom, I have to go. Please forgive me. I have to do this alone. I need to know why this happened, and my visions will tell me. Don't follow me or try to find me. I kept secrets from you and Mom. Not only can I see visions since the whitefish day, but I can speak without words to anyone. I love you.

Now to get to Kathy's house. A bus pulled up outside the hotel and Chloe hopped on it.

***

"Kathy, come on out." Chloe yelled up

towards her window. Kathy looked out the window and saw her best friend down below. Within seconds, Kathy came running out the door to see Chloe. The two had adventures like one wouldn't believe two girls could have, and were always talking about boys. Well, mostly Kathy talked about boys and Chloe just nodded her head in agreement. Kathy never made Chloe feel like she was a weirdo, despite what the kids in school would say. In fact, Kathy even dressed like Chloe at times to make her feel better.

"There's no danger, Kathy. Let's go up to the hill and watch the cars from the freeway."

"Okay, Chloe. Maybe we'll see Greg again. He is so cute. Can he hang out with us?" Chloe rolled her eyes but she knew how much Kathy liked Greg. Greg was one of the boys that teased Chloe, but she'd never told Kathy. Her muscles tightened in her stomach, but she loved Kathy.

Chloe smirked but nodded, and then they were off. They made it to the hill in a short while and began to watch the cars. Chloe seemed occupied, as if she was looking for something. Kathy seemed to notice a change in her friend, but remained silent until she couldn't stand it anymore.

"Chloe, what's wrong? You said you needed

to talk. You sure are acting strange today."

Chloe bit her tongue and silently argued with herself over whether or not to tell Kathy. Chloe and her mother were never separated. She could still picture her mother's beautiful smile, but her last memory of her was that she was feeling helpless when it came to Chloe receiving this damn gift. Part of Chloe resented the fact that she was a witch because the cost was so high.

Exhaling deeply, Chloe started to cry and let it out. She told Kathy all about the horror from the night before.

***

Tom woke up suddenly in a fear that he couldn't shake. Calming himself for a minute, he quickly jumped into the shower. The night before had made him feel dirty and ashamed that he couldn't protect his Marlene or beautiful Chloe. As he showered, his mind opened and he recalled Chloe's words. He couldn't believe what she had done…she'd left.

Turning off the water, he rushed to get dressed and began his search for Chloe. He didn't really know Seattle as much as he knew Yakima. But, honestly, how hard could it be? He tried to imagine himself being a young tween and a witch who was separated from her mother for the first time. Thinking about his little Chloe, he came to the realization that she would have gone back to familiar surroundings. Maybe not her home, but close enough. Friends in the neighborhood? Perhaps.

He had his car brought to him and rushed back to their neighborhood. Driving through the streets up and down, he decided this was not the most intelligent way to track the powerful little witch. Stopping the car, he allowed his mind to search out for Chloe's aura. Tom chuckled as he realized that there was still so much to teach the little witch. His blue aura canvased the neighborhood and he found her. She was with another child.

Sweet child. You can't run from this. I have to teach you so much more. Chloe, you can be safe. Come back to me.

He hoped that Chloe would recognize his aura and let herself receive his message. Now, all he could do was wait.

***

Kabos managed to find a place to sleep and gather his thoughts. He had to find the one that was prophesized. The child of spirits. Through her, it was proclaimed that there would be a powerful one that would be of two races. Two races that needed to merge but weren't supposed to. Kabos had left Michael and Marcus instructions for his personal and business affairs…affairs that did not include the Avalani. He couldn't let them destroy what he'd been working on.

He knew he should sleep but found his thoughts racing about the prophecy. He recalled what the parchment read about the Witch's Prophecy. Having seen it only once for a brief moment, he had memorized as much as he could.

The seers will have a chosen one. A child. She will grow in strength and wisdom despite her age. When she reaches her full potential, her heart will be torn between two…the seers and the cold ones. Love will be her answer and guide. Her colors will change and her decisions will forsake one for the other. Wisdom and justice will be her strength and courage. Through her, a scepter will be born. The instrument that will seal the fate of the queen.

Kabos could not recall the rest because he was so tired. He needed to sleep before the night came. Then it was time to feed. He had to get to her before Gerard and his bastard servants found the girl.

CHAPTER SIX
KIDNAPPED

Kathy knew her friend was strange, but this was the first time she really thought Chloe had lost it. She had never seen Chloe just stand there and tell such a tale.

"Chloe, this can't be real. This is just too weird—even for you. Look, I'm your friend and all, but really? Some evil creature came and knocked your mom out cold? And you are going to be the most powerful witch the world has been waiting for? Seriously Chloe, if the world heard of such a prophecy, don't you think we'd all be helping?"

Kathy stared at Chloe in disbelief. She was beginning to think the kids in school were right. Chloe was a strange duck. There were things such as standing up for your friend, but to now believe she was a witch? Kathy wasn't sure anymore, but Chloe never lied to her.

"I'm telling you the truth, Kat. I would never lie to you. Watch this. I'll show you a spell." And she did.

Kathy's eyes grew wide in amazement but she kept quiet. She was intrigued and in shock at the same time. But in her heart, she believed her best friend, and that's all that should mattert?

***

Overlooking the hill, Chloe could see the Space Needle, one of her favorite places. It reached high into the sky and was surrounded by the city of Seattle. To her, it seemed like the city was swallowing the Needle. Every time she and her mom had gone to the Seattle Center, Chloe always had to make sure that she went to the top of the Needle. The gift store was always one of her favorite places. Inside the Seattle Center, stores also piqued her interest. Some of her favorite times at the Center were when they would have festivals or events. It would get crazy with all the Seattle people, or friendlies, as she called them. Seattle was beginning to be her favorite place in the world, although she dreamed of a life without her powers at times. Now she dreamed of having her mother back.

Chloe stared off into space for what seemed like an eternity. She didn't hear Kathy talking to her. Her visions took over. This time her vision was different. She was talking to a young man, maybe in his twenties, with dark hair. His clothes were simple, jeans and a shirt. He was leaning over a body and she could see his face. He was handsome, but on the corner of his mouth dripped a trail of red blood. Another person was near him, a blond man, and looking closer, she could see that they were both in Seattle because the Needle was in the background. It was as if the dark haired man was looking right at her, though she knew he wasn't. She could see his fangs. Oh my god! A vampire in Seattle.

"Chloe, did you hear me? I'm worried about you. Why don't you stay with us? Chloe?"

Minutes passed and Chloe didn't respond. She didn't see that Kathy had left her. Chloe continued to look over the hill and continued with her visions. Hours passed.

Dark was approaching and Chloe still remained at the hill. The wind became cooler, yet she wasn't cold. She felt dizzy like she had the night before. Her head became flustered, her fingers tingled, and blue sparks started to sizzle but faded quickly. Chloe remained on her feet, steadfast. The ground started to shake a little, the leaves crunched underneath the sound of boots. The stranger came closer and Chloe remained silent, unmoving. For some reason, she couldn't speak or call for help to come and save her.

***

The stranger could feel her power, yet Chloe never moved. She looked like a teenage girl, not a woman yet. How could this child be the one? Next thing he knew, she collapsed and fell to the earth. He didn't expect the girl to faint. This was not typical. Normally, witches had dizzy spells but never fainted. Still, the stranger moved closer, but slowly. He sensed another witch around, but he couldn't see anyone.

Kabos bent down and picked up the long haired witch in his strong arms. She was smaller than he'd thought she would be, younger too. The girl wore her hair straight and long. Her bangs covered most of her face, but there was a sense of feistiness in this girl. For a teen, she was pretty. She had those red pouty lips and was dressed all in black. Kabos didn't understand the girls of today, always wearing black.

He carried the girl witch to his car. Once he

got there, he placed her in the trunk and sped the car in the direction of the estate. He didn't want her in the car with him because he was afraid, afraid of her power. In the books of prophecy, there was a warning about this witch.

***

Tom eyed the street carefully but never saw anything. He toyed with the idea that he should mentally connect with Chloe, but something kept telling him not to. He watched and waited. In the rearview mirror he saw a car coming in his direction, but there was only one person in the driver's seat from what he could see. He waited. Senses were telling him so many different things that he was losing faith in his abilities.

That was until he saw him. It was that damn vampire, Kabos. The coven talked about how one vampire longed to fulfill the Blood Prophecy, but all the coven cared about was the Witch's Prophecy. Damn stinky vampire.

Then he felt it...another presence. The presence of a witch. But Chloe was nowhere to be seen. Or was she with the vampire somehow?

Tom decided to start the engine and follow the car as it sped away.

***

47

Chloe regained consciousness in the trunk of a moving car. She began to feel scared and lost without her mother and Tom. She didn't know what to do. But as she closed her eyes, she reached within her for her power. Tom had been teaching this technique to her for the last year and a half. According to the books that Tom let her read, Chloe was a descendant from the Witches of Salem, but they hadn't gotten far in teaching her the details. Her breathing slowed and became steady. Her body temperature maintained an even balance as she felt her power stirring. Her power felt warm as it travelled through her blood, and in the pit of her stomach, she felt butterflies. Chloe continued to reach down further and further until her body started to shake. Her fingers clutched at her shirt and her toes curled as the power rose from the pit of her stomach outward. The trunk, as dark as it was, was covered in blue light, and the lid of the trunk flew open as fire emerged from the car and reached to the night sky.

Chloe sat up in the trunk, fully aware of her power. She looked in the direction of the street and saw a car following, and recognized the plate...it was Tom. Thank God he'd come for her. His Corvette was trying to stay close, but for some reason it kept swerving. She tried to think of one of the spells that she learned not that long ago, but her head was really hurting. When she fainted, she hit her head hard on the edge of the trunk.

Trying the relaxation methods, Chloe tried to find her inner strength and peace. Closing her eyes, biting her bottom lip, and taking a deep breath, she was able to recall the spell that would grab hold of a moving object and pull them closer, kind of like a tractor beam. It was such a cool spell when she and her cousin Rae had played around with it. Thinking about Rae made her smile. Rae was a cute preschooler, but also a strong witch.

***

Tom watched in disbelief as the trunk lid flew open and landed on the side of the road. He saw his sweet Chloe sitting up, staring right at him. A goldish aura seemed to outline her body form, and even from that distance, Tom could see her once dark eyes were now silver. "Oh sweet Jesus. What power did she receive now?"

The car continued to give chase to the fleeing car. Tom had to decide what to do next. He had no idea what he was up against. Just then, his phone rang. He had no time nor patience for distractions. Before he knew it, another car was coming upon him at a very fast pace. He couldn't go any faster, but the car behind him started closing in on him.

Suddenly, Tom's car took a hit from behind, causing him to swerve. His hands gripped the steering wheel and tried to counter the swaying, but no matter how hard he tried, he couldn't regain control. His car swerved to the right and hit a tree. A loud crashing sound was all Tom heard as his head hit the wheel. Blood trickled down his forehead and he just mumbled, "Chloe" before passing out.

***

Having felt the car's trunk open violently, the vampire swerved the car and became unnerved at this little witch. He began to grind his teeth, curl his lips, and tried to focus on pulling over. He had to contain the witch long enough to get to the estate. Once out of the car, he stretched his back, cracked his knuckles, and moved to the trunk. Inside, he saw her. She was a pretty little girl. But with such power, he knew his kind didn't stand a chance.

Kabos reached in the trunk and tried to grab the girl.

***

Suddenly, Chloe experienced her visions once more and the vampire was thrown back. He landed on the road flat on his back. In her vision, Chloe saw the redhead again.

The woman with the headband crossed the bridge, running hard, heading down the dirt road. She was going to turn right but stopped in her tracks. Hands on her thighs, she hunched over and took a deep breath. A crazy thing to do in the middle of a run, but then she continued to run on. She is a beautiful lady, Chloe thought. The vision disappeared and Chloe closed her eyes, drained of energy from the vision.

CHAPTER SEVEN
FEAR

Chloe opened her eyes and found herself laying on a couch, bound and gagged. Her first thoughts were of fear and death, but something inside her kept her calm. It was as if a voice from the past was calling to her.

Chloe, child. There is nothing to fear but fear itself. This vampire will not hurt you, but seeks to find what you know. Through the vast space of time, the prophecy is born. Feel what you feel, know what you know. Don't let the dead ones turn you from the path you were born to. Sleep now and let the dreams show you the way.

Chloe took a deep breath, as much as she was able to with the gag around her mouth, and drifted into slumber. Again, images filled her mind. Images of battles, blood, vampires feeding on humans, large dogs standing next to the redheaded woman again. Who was she? Chloe let her mind continue to drift as she lay in the trance like sleep state.

She could hear him enter the room. She was dizzy because he was near. *Damn vampire*, thought Chloe. Chloe could hear the footsteps coming closer. The boots were heavy and every step seemed to stimulate a new fear in her. Tom and her mother had never prepared her for something like this. It was just pure craziness. One minute she was a normal kid, and now she was missing or kidnapped, whatever they wanted to call it. All because of some prophecy, some stupid prophecy of a redhead lady. Still, with the reassurance from the voice she heard, she maintained her trance-like state. *Better to let him think I am still out*, she thought.

***

Kabos reached the girl and stroked her hair. She was pretty, and he could definitely feel the power in her. He didn't speak to her. Instead, he spoke to the person who had just entered the room. Ah, his son's son. Marcus. Marcus looked at the girl on the couch but didn't say a word. Instead, Kabos used their minds to communicate.

Marcus, fledgling. This is the witch, but she is not ready to do what must be done. In fact, I believe we are too early. How goes things with Michael?

Kabos, things go well. It's the waiting that's driving us insane with the prophecy. But this girl, she's really cute for a kid.

Stop that or feel my wrath. She is not to be harmed in any way. Kabos did not smile, but shot a strong glare of warning towards Marcus. Marcus did not continue.

***

Chloe slowly began to think of the charms that would remove her bindings. Little by little the ropes started to undo themselves. The gag became less restrictive against her mouth, allowing her to speak. Suddenly, a voice that was not hers broke the silence, and she looked at the vampire and his accomplice. She could see them shift in uncertainty.

"Foolish dead ones. The child is protected by a prophecy older than you. You cannot seek your answers through her. She will hold the key in years to come, but not soon enough. Through her comes a friendship that will bind your kind to another and another. You cannot destroy what it is you seek. Her memories are limited. She will love one of your kind, and her future is writ."

Her eyes opened and she saw Kabos and another cute man fall to the floor. The vampires were on all fours, screaming curses about the prophecy. Chloe felt sorry for them. Maybe they didn't like the prophecy either. What the hell was with the prophecy?

***

Tom regained consciousness and leaned his head back to assess his current predicament. His right hand reached into the console and brought out a handkerchief, which he used to dab the dripping blood from his forehead. Glancing at his watch, he realized that he was only unconscious for about an hour. Moving his legs slightly, and then his left arm, Tom realized that he wasn't paralyzed. *Thank God*, he thought.

He knew he had to find Chloe. He'd lost an hour, but he could still track them. Tracking was his special gift, but not because he was a witch. No one knew his secret, not even Marlene. It was an abomination to be mixed, but Tom could not change his parentage no matter the cost or the times he'd attempted to. Eventually he learned to accept it. It is what it is, as they said.

Glancing up, he could see the lights of the

ambulance, the police cars, and more. People were all outside trying to assess his situation. Tom slowly opened the car door and stood up. People gasped as they saw him. Except for a few scratches, there was not a single injury on him. Tom smiled.

"I'm okay folks. I was hit from behind and lost control of my car. I do need to find my child. She's been taken."

***

The sheriff somehow felt that this man was telling the truth. He listened as Tom told him how Chloe was in the trunk of a car that was speeding away. Calling it in, the sheriff put his officers on the lookout, but it wasn't clear how far they could've gotten by now. Running his hand through his dark hair, Sheriff Frank Jamieson did not know what to do. He believed Tom, but knowing the roads, there were so many places the abductor could be by now. An hour could prove to be long enough to disappear.

"Tom, let's get you to the hospital to get checked out. I've got my men searching. Chloe will be our top priority. Plus, I think you and I need to have a private conversation. Don't you?"

The sheriff moved closer to Tom, allowing

Tom to see the mark of the coven. Tom glanced at the sheriff and nodded.

***

Tom and the sheriff spoke quietly away from listening ears. He filled the sheriff in on Chloe's disappearance and the strange occurrences that had transpired in the last couple of days. He noticed that the sheriff nodded and acknowledged what he said.

"Tom, you know I don't question what happened. But, how in the hell did you survive this crash? Where's Marlene now? You know we are all supposed to protect the mother of the greatest witch at any cost. No human, no witch could've survived such a crash. It's incredible, but I still have to explain it in the report, Tom. Tell me."

He couldn't explain about his true nature, not to anyone. He'd promised his mother long ago that this secret would die with him. How was he supposed to explain that while he may be a witch, he was also something more? Tom just smiled and told the sheriff he thought Chloe might have cast a protection spell on him so he could find her. He had to leave and told the sheriff he had to go.

The sheriff, much to the dismay of his

officers, let him go in pursuit of Chloe, but only if he went with him. So, the two men sped down the road in search of Chloe.

CHAPTER EIGHT
DESTINY

Kabos unbound Chloe and gripped her by her long hair. Even if she was the witch the prophecy spoke of, there was no reason he couldn't instill a slight touch of fear in her. Maybe that would trigger the voice to come back. He had questions and he needed answers. Pulling her head back so that her eyes could only stare at the ceiling, Kabos hunched over her so that her view became only of his face.

"Child witch, I promise you that no harm will come to you unless you don't call forward that voice. If you don't, things will not be so promising or uneventful for you. Sweet child, bring forth the voice of the past, the future all in one...NOW!"

He knew that his loud voice would scare

the child, and that was his intention. Normally Kabos didn't scream or behave violently, but he wanted to have Michael's path set up so that Kabos could meet the sun. He was tired of living as a vampire and not seeing the end of the Avalani. He hated Gerard with the greatest hatred his dead black heart could hold.

Kabos sensed that Marcus was not feeling too good about this, but at least that whelp had the good sense to remain quiet. The girl started to cry but remained silent. She didn't scream. She definitely showed courage, Kabos would give her that. The girl's eyes showed fear and determination, but something more. *Ah yes*, he thought. There it is. The sight. The girl has the sight.

***

Chloe tried to hold back her inner voice, but alas, she could no longer control what was happening to her. Her body arched back even further than the force Kabos held onto her hair with. Her fingers clawed at the floor, trying to find something to hold onto, but failed. Her breathing came faster, and suddenly, a blue light shone around her form.

"Heed me, dead ones. You think to force this child of the prophecy to submit to your will? Foolish vampires. Yes, I know who you are. You may not know of me, but I know you. Idiot Kabos and the emotional Marcus. You think that that prophecy does not know who its players are? Why do you rush the role this child plays? She is not full into her power yet until her eighteenth birthday. But mark the words once more, vampires.

"A day will come when the reckoning awaits vampires, witches, werewolves. The redheaded queen will unite with the raven haired witch. Both will be bound to your sons, Kabos, through love and hate, emotion and conflict, but a child of unification will be birthed by this raven haired girl. A child whose wings will tell the fate of the prophecy. Protect this girl, do not scare her. She is one of the chosen ones. The prophecy will yield its fate upon the chosen ones' sacrifices."

As soon as Chloe finished and the spirit left her body, she collapsed to the floor. Tears rolled down her cheeks and she fell asleep.

***

Kabos let the child go and left her asleep on the floor. Motioning for Marcus to follow him into another room, he closed the door behind them. The last thing he wanted was to take a chance and have the witch child hear them. He slammed his fist on the table in a rage that Marcus had never seen before. Marcus had no idea what made him so furious.

"Kabos, you need to calm down."

"Don't tell me to calm down, vampire. It is I who made you and Michael what you are today. It is because of me that you are prepared for what must be. But a child will be birthed by this witch? There is nothing written in the prophecy that we have yet on this. Pure lies."

Marcus had never seen this side of Kabos, and in fact, it scared him. Both he and Michael had always been groomed for the prophecy to find the queen, to make her, but not to scare little girls. This was preposterous. But he was the son, or grandson by mortal terms, and obedient. Marcus was the kind of soul that had never lost his humanity despite being a vampire. He knew he had to contact Michael, but first, there was something about this girl. He felt a connection…a distant connection, but there was something there.

Kabos retired to another room to think and left Marcus to watch the girl. Marcus obeyed, as usual. He approached the sleeping girl on the floor, bent down, and enveloped her in his arms. She was light as a feather and her long hair tickled his arm. Gently he laid her down on the couch and brushed her hair back from her face. Her pale face had a sense of tranquility, but Marcus noticed something strange. The tears did not stop flowing. In fact, they kept streaming down her cheek, but they were not clear tears... they were a translucent blue. Marcus touched her tear and rubbed his index finger and thumb together. Strange. It wasn't wet as it should be, but it was something he couldn't explain.

The girl moaned but her eyes remained closed. Leaning closer to her mouth, something compelled him to kiss her, but before he could touch her lips, her right hand reached up to him and pulled him closer to her. Her eyes flared open.

"You. You are the one that will bind yourself to this witch. Through you and her will come a winged child. A child with purpose. Keep the secret guarded that it is you she will choose. Lovers will come and go, but your heart will be bound to hers for eternity. She will love no one else but you. Together, the child will be the instrument the queen will use to turn the tides of the prophecy toward good. But evil will reign and friends may become enemies. Evil will be in those closest to you as well as your enemies. It is you who must prevail. The queen will surpass evil, but only with the child. Run, sweet vampire. Run and return this child."

The girl fell back and closed her eyes once more. She was asleep still.

Marcus knew he couldn't tell Kabos what he'd just witnessed. Quietly, he thought about what to do. In a moment, his life had been turned upside down. But, he decided to listen to the voice he'd heard from the girl. He picked her up and carried her to his car. Laying her gently in the back seat, he covered her with a blanket. Climbing into the front seat, he took out his keys and began to start the car. Marcus hoped that Kabos wouldn't hear him leave.

The car crept slowly down the road until Marcus was sure they were in the clear. First chance he got, he revved up the engine and sped away.

***

Tom and the sheriff continued on the road and saw the car coming towards them at a fast speed. A young, dark haired man was driving, and there was no one else in the car with him that they could see. But the hairs on both men's arms stood up, and their senses began to tell them a vampire was nearby. The only person that they saw was the man driving in the opposite direction of where they were headed. The sheriff gripped the wheel and made a left turn to follow the car. Looking at each other, both men could tell they were onto something.

Tom told the sheriff, "Don't lose him. He must have her."

The sheriff said, "We'll find her, Tom. She is under the protection of the coven. No harm will come to the sweet girl. Then we need to reassess what the hell is going on."

Tom agreed. His mind wandered to thoughts of Marlene, but he wasn't too worried because of the protection spell he'd placed on her...worried, but not a lot.

The car continued to follow the vampire's car, and eventually they were right behind it.

***

Marcus noticed the police car behind him and decided to pull over. The last thing he needed was a chase with law enforcement. Looking in the mirror, he saw that the girl was still asleep. She had black hair, he had dark hair. Maybe she could pass as his younger sister or something. Taking a deep breath, he tried to collect his thoughts of how he was going to play this out.

He steered the car gently to the right side of the road, put his hazards on, and let it idle. He rolled down the window and was preparing his story. Marcus noticed the sheriff and another man approaching. *This can't be good*, he thought.

"What seems to be the problem, deputy?"

"Sir, you know what the problem is." The sheriff looked in the backseat and saw the young girl in the back. "Tom, is that Chloe?"

The other man looked and nodded.

Marcus was not sure what the hell was going on but he opened the door, and as he did the men stepped back, but only enough to let him out. He tried not to bare his fangs, though he wanted to. Remembering what the voice had told him, he began to blurt out the story that was told to him. The sheriff and the other man just listened. There was no fighting. Marcus was prepared for a fight, but instead he managed to gain their attention. Perhaps even their sympathy.

Tom told Marcus that he understood and he believed him.

"Look, I only wanted to bring the girl home, but I didn't know where she lived. I had to do this while Kabos was in the other room.

She…she spoke about the future. I kind of feel attached to her."

Running his hand through his thick hair, he didn't know what else to say. The men opened the door and took Chloe from the backseat. As they touched her, she began to speak again.

"No harm will come to the one who is mine. My heart will bind to his. He is to be my mate, my connection."

Marcus looked at Tom and spoke. "This is what I mean. She says these things, but won't wake up. She also had a pretty bad scare, and her tears…well, aren't normal tears. But, the sun is coming. I must go. You know my nature and I know yours, witches."

Marcus returned to the car and sped off, leaving the two men and the girl behind. But as he drove away, he was surprised that he missed the girl, even though they'd never spoken to each other. She was in his thoughts. But something was pulling at him. He turned the car around and went right back to the spot where he delivered the girl to them. They were still there.

He quickly got out, hoping to speak fast and long enough for them to understand before the sun came up.

"Here's my number. Keep it secret. Call me when night falls. I want to help the girl and have information. Please. There's a strange connection and it involves the prophecy, but the sun is coming up. Please."

Marcus, feeling relieved, left and went back to Kabos as soon as possible.

CHAPTER NINE
RAGE

Later that night, Chloe continued to sleep but her mind was awake. Images, flashes, and dreams filled her mind. She kept seeing the redheaded woman, a dark haired man, a blond haired man, and what appeared to be an older version of herself. Then, she saw the same woman with large looking dogs and a very old woman, who wore a triangle tattoo on her forehead. At least it looked like a tattoo. Chloe stirred and moaned. Though her eyes couldn't open, she knew Tom had found her. She didn't know how, but he had.

Hearing his voice soothed her. She was scared that she couldn't open her eyes, but finally she heard him speak to another man.

"Sheriff, should we call that vampire? He

71

seemed good and genuine, especially if he was trying to save my Chloe. I just know we have to get back to Marlene. My protection spell is only going to last so long."

"I know, Tom. Let's call him, but I'll get a burner phone. This way he can't trace it. Not that I think he would, but if this is about the prophecy, we need to be extra careful."

Chloe made another attempt to open her eyes. The images she was seeing now burned in her mind. She would never forget the woman's looks. Moaning louder caused Tom and the sheriff to run to her side. She sensed they were near.

Finally her eyes opened and the first person she looked at was Tom. She hugged him in sheer joy.

"Tom, I was so scared. They didn't hurt me, except I think I said some strange things. What the hell is going on?"

"Sweetheart, normally I don't like that language you use, but it's okay right now. Come here and give me a hug."

While she hugged Tom, her eyes watched the other man call someone. He was a stranger to her, but she decided to let Tom go and stood up. Going over to the stranger, she lightly touched the tail of his jacket. More images flooded through her, but these were much more soothing than the images she was seeing earlier. Images of a young boy wearing a cowboy hat and riding on a man's shoulders, laughing. He was so happy. Looking at the boy's face, she saw that it was a kid version of the stranger.

***

The phone rang four times before the vampire picked it up. The sheriff was patient but spoke to the vampire. "Please hold. I'm putting Tom on."

Silence was on the other end.

"This is Tom. Which vampire are you?"

There was a brief pause.

"I'm Marcus. The girl. Is she all right?"

"Yes, Marcus. She's resilient and brave. Explain your cryptic message. We don't have all night. Her mother...uh, she needs to go home to her mother."

The sheriff listened as close as he could to what the vampire had to say to Tom. But for five minutes, there was nothing but heavy breathing.

***

Tom was beginning to get impatient and he felt that it was beginning to show to Chloe.

He never let her see him impatient, even in his teachings to her. But, this was beyond infuriating.

Marcus began to speak.

"What I have to say, please let me say. Ask your questions after so I don't lose what she said. The girl. She is a witch. Probably the one the prophecy speaks of. I'm sure you witches have heard about The Blood Prophecy. It speaks of a powerful witch. But, pages are missing from the Vampire Prophecy about that. The girl spoke, yet it was not in her voice. She will love a vampire and he will love her. I don't understand how, but the union will bring a child. That child belongs with the queen. That's the basics of what she said."

Tom was boiling mad. His even colored cheeks turned red and he tried hard to keep his voice low.

"What do you mean, love a vampire? A child? That can't be. No vampire can father a child."

"I know, but it is prophesized, and here's the strange part…I am that vampire."

"Whaaat? Absurd. Absolutely not. This cannot happen. You kidnapped her."

"No, I did not. But Kabos did. The maker

74

of my maker kidnapped her. I guess you could say he's my grandfather, so to speak. I don't understand it either, but she's just a child. I'm hundreds of years old."

Tom had heard all he could stand and disconnected the phone. He was done. Looking at the sheriff, he whispered so Chloe couldn't hear. "We're going home to Yakima. To the coven, after we pick up her mother. They will be safer there. Chloe will be safe."

"What did he say, Tom? Tell me. I have a right to know."

Tom looked closely at him. "Chloe and this vampire will be a couple and have a child. We must prevent this. We have to leave now."

The sheriff nodded in agreement. "Such unifications must never happen. Tell me where to take you and I'll drive."

CHAPTER TEN
PROPHECY

The three powerful witches were driving towards Chloe's mother. They knew that they had to get there because the protection spell would only last so long. The sheriff drove with the lights on knowing it would get them there the fastest.

"Tom, you really should know my first name now that we're in this together. Call me Frank."

"All right. Frank it is. Thank you for helping."

Frank had reddish brown hair with brown eyes that seemed so gentle for an officer of the law. His glasses framed his face perfectly, and there was not a blemish anywhere on his skin. He seemed to carry an air of positivity with him everywhere he went. Chloe noticed how he constantly glanced in the rearview mirror, always checking on her. He'd already asked her four times if she needed to stop, was cold, or anything. Her answer was always that she was fine.

However, this one last time he looked in the mirror, Chloe wasn't looking at him. She was looking at the sky. Her hand accidentally touched his jacket that was laying on the backseat, and images appeared of Frank. Her hand cringed while she shivered at the sight. This man had gone through a rough patch in his career. Seeing the images brought tears to her eyes, but she hid her face from the men.

Before she could think about something else, her body started to shake. Closing her eyes, she let the premonitions fill her mind. These were her visions. Her gift. A nauseous feeling also came over her with a strange smell.

Moments later, the visions were gone. Chloe screamed. It must have scared Frank and Tom because before she knew it, the car swerved and almost crashed. But it didn't.

***

"What the hell Chloe? Are you hurt?" Tom was shouting at her.

"No, it was just...the visions, you know. These were horrible."

"Take a deep breath, Chloe. Once you can, tell us about the visions."

Chloe relaxed her mind and body, using the techniques that Tom had taught her since she was a little girl. Her body was calm now.

"The visions were of a man. He was strange, but he was human, or looked human. He wears a hat, but he is standing over a large dog. I don't know what kind of dog. But the man has a sword. Men are coming towards him, but he won't leave his dog. He looks weird. I don't like how he looks. But in my vision, he looked up directly, as if he could see me. Tom, it was super creepy."

Before she could continue, Chloe's hands clasped the sides of her head and she screamed. It was such a shrill shriek that it once again scared Frank and Tom. Next thing she knew, her world became black.

***

Tom leaned over the seat and tried to shake Chloe. Her face, once pale, was now turning blue. She wasn't getting oxygen, or so he thought, but he could feel her breathing. Her body was in a trance like state. She wasn't dying. Thank God! His sweet Chloe. Then, it dawned on him. She was using her powers or receiving new ones. One could never tell until it was complete.

Suddenly, her voice called out.

"Do not fear me, witches of the coven chosen for the prophecy. Through this child, powers will transform her soul, mind, and body. She will be one of the strongest witches in all time, descendant of Sarah Good. Her gifts will be immeasurable, but her heart must remain pure. Heed the words of the prophecy.

"The witch will be the right arm of the queen, the defender of the prophecy. The child of the witch will be fathered by a blood drinker, yet she will be more. Armed with a sword and a band of believers, the witch, her child, and the queen will be the truest weapons of justice. It is up to the witch to defend her heart and be true.

"Guard the life of the witch, protect the body of the witch, and be true to the prophecy. Seek what you must find. Go back to the beginning to protect the witch. More will come for her."

Tom looked at Chloe, who remained in a deep slumber. The girl had been through so much in the last several days that he urged Frank to drive faster. The car raced along the road and eventually they found themselves staring at Marlene. The protection spell had worn off. She was sitting up in bed as Tom carried Chloe in his arms.

Marlene just stared at Tom in silence and nodded. Tom knew he would have explaining to do.

***

Marlene motioned for Tom to put Chloe on the bed. She had risen in less than three blinks and watched as her daughter lay silently in the bed she'd just occupied. Her daughter's body was in a witch trance, something so rare that only the most special of witches went through it. It was something that covens revered because only a handful of witches had that ability. Marlene recognized it immediately because she was the historian of the coven, and recalled reading about Sarah Good. But what she read about Sarah was never in the history books the schoolchildren learned.

"Tom, it's okay. You did right by her. It only proves that our Chloe is the one that has been chosen. She's the one from the books. What happened? I only remember a force knocking me down."

Tom was quiet and then looked at Frank.

Before she realized it, both men started talking at once, spilling everything. Marlene was good at deciphering men, especially Tom, and was able to put it all together based on what they shared. She was not expecting the involvement of vampires so soon, but it mattered not anymore. What was done was done.

Marlene left and ran to the attic. All their witch books were kept in the attic so that Chloe could have a normal life...well, a normal life as much as possible. She found the trunk that she'd hidden from Chloe's eyes because of its contents. Taking the key from her pocket, she unlocked it. With a slight tug at the lock, it gave way and Marlene lifted the lid. Inside the trunk was a very old book, a bright red silk cloth that hid a unique dagger, and other items. Reaching for the book, she lifted it and blew off the dust remnants. On the cover was the mark of the witches. Saying her prayer of the coven, she held the book close to her chest.

Marlene found the rocking chair in a corner and sat down. Turning page after page, she skimmed the spells, the history, and things in search of anything related to the Blood Prophecy. She saw it. Closing the book, she returned to the others.

"I found it. I think I did."
Showing them, she began to read.

CHAPTER ELEVEN
MERGE

Chloe remained awake in her mind but her body was asleep. There were no more visions, no premonitions, nothing. But there was a voice pulling at her. A voice from the past. Holding onto her strong sense of who she was, she listened as the voice continued to talk to her.

Prepare the path that awaits you, witch. A bargain was made centuries ago. You are the vessel of my beloved Sarah. She will rise once more to walk the earth, but through you will be her powers. Invoke her spirit into yours and the two of you will be united. My Sarah will be silent as you grow, but her powers will infuse with yours, making you stronger. Making you my vessel now. Sleep child. Sleep well. But in time, you will come into your powers. Sarah's powers. You will be mine. You will reap the benefits

85

from Sarah for her return. You will be my consort, and finally we will turn the tides of the prophecy.

Chloe continued to listen but the voice stopped. Instead she felt another spirit enter her body and try to connect with her. She welcomed this new spirit because it felt familiar to her. In her mind, she spoke to the new spirit.

I'm Chloe, descendant of Sarah Good, chosen one of the prophecy.

Yes, sweet Chloe. I'm Sarah, your ancestor. Blessed be. Open your mind to me. Your body accepts me, but I need your mind to accept me. Vengeance upon the cruelty of others is mine to give. You are my shell, my host to make it happen. Merge with me and we'll become one. We will be forever formidable. We will serve the Dark One.

Her body opened itself by force because Sarah was so much stronger. Her mind began to open and bind its will to her. Chloe could not resist it no matter how hard she tried. In the end, Chloe and Sarah merged, and as their two beings became one, a blue light encompassed Chloe's body and brightened the room.

Chloe could hear the others in the room but she could not communicate with them. After what seemed like an eternity, she opened her eyes.

"It is done. Summon the coven."

Then her eyes rolled back into her head.

***

Marlene opened the book once more. She said the incantation to protect her daughter. She noticed that Tom was on the phone and she guessed that he was calling the coven. Marlene wanted to help Chloe, and the only way she knew how was with the coven.

"Tom, Frank. We need to get her to the coven now."

Tom and Frank nodded and told her that they thought the same thing. Marlene took that moment to pack her and Chloe's bags while the men kept watch. She came back in less than fifteen minutes with bags and witch books, ready to move.

Frank gently picked up Chloe and they left in Marlene's SUV. Tom slid behind the wheel while Frank rode shotgun. Marlene sat in the back with Chloe's head on her lap. She stroked Chloe's hair with one hand while the other held the books. She tried to read one of the books looking for a spell or something to explain what was happening. She found nothing.

***

As they drove to Yakima, Frank kept watch.

His hands gripped his shotgun tightly as he scanned the surroundings. Not wanting to raise any suspicions, Tom kept the car at a steady pace. They drove for a few hours and finally arrived in Yakima.

"Frank, help Marlene. I'm going to find the members of the council and see if we can share with them what we learned. We are going to need all the help we can get."

Frank nodded and started to open the car door. At the same moment, Tom was already more than halfway into the building. Marlene got out after Frank lifted Chloe from the backseat. As he picked her up, Chloe started having convulsions. An unseen force caused him to lose his balance, and Marlene barely caught them.

"Winds of calm, winds of peace. Make this child slumber with a gentle breeze."

Marlene repeated the incantation once more to make sure that Chloe just slept in peace, no more convulsions, and no more distractions.

***

The coven leader appeared at the door and ushered them inside. There was no time for formalities. She needed to know what was happening to this child.

"Come, come. Bring her inside. Hurry. And of course, welcome!"

Marija was the coven leader at this time. She took her rightful place after accepting the position from the previous leader. She came from the Du Loux family line, which was not quite as long as Marlene's family's, but their matriarch was one of the heretic witches after the Salem Witch Trials.

Chloe was placed in her own personal rooms and attended to by personal attendants. Marija may not be royalty, but being the coven leader was quite similar. Marija called Tom to join her and ordered Marlene to rest.

Tom and Marija were examining Chloe's state before she spoke.

"Tom, we need to finish the merge spell. It seems that the child is open to merging, but there is a small part of her that is resisting at all costs. This is causing her powers to break down. It may look like she's succeeding and getting new powers, but in reality, she isn't. It is difficult for her because she is so young. Do you remember the merge spell?"

Tom nodded and had that look of worry in his eye. He began to say the merge spell, forcing Chloe to accept the merge regardless of the resistance.

Marija noticed that Chloe's body was fighting Tom. *That girl is strong!*

Joining her power with Tom's, the two of them spoke the words of the merge spell. With both their powers, they were able to force the spell to work. In response, Chloe's body calmed down and her mind was completely open. It was at that moment that Marija took her hand and rested her palm on Chloe's forehead. She simply told her mind to open, and she was immediately connected to Chloe's mind.

"Child, accept whatever is given to you by the powers that be. It is your destiny, your burden for being so special. Accept."

Chloe's body did one last convulsion and the merge was now complete. Sarah Good and Chloe were now one.

***

Hours later Chloe woke from the trance and sat up in the bed. Her face was back to its pale complexion, but she placed her hands in front of her face and was examining them as if seeing them for the first time. Through her eyes she didn't recognize the people in front of her, including the woman standing by her. In fact, it wasn't Chloe looking through her eyes, it was

Sarah Good.

This place, this room was strange. It didn't have the feel of Salem that she remembered. But then it hit her...she had been killed for being a witch. How long had it been? She wanted to ask but was afraid. Finally, Chloe's voice reassured her that all was well. The two had become one, and it was now two who looked out through their eyes.

Chloe managed to come to the surface and speak. "How did I get here?"

Marlene smiled and found a cool compress for her forehead.

"It's okay, sweet, sweet Chloe. We're back at the coven. You underwent a transformation or something. What do you recall?"

"Mom. This is weird. It's like there are two of me in my body. But I feel whole for the first time. Tom! Tom! I'm glad you are here too! Thank you, thank you!"

Tom and Frank smiled at her and remained on guard. Marlene just kept pampering her the way a mother should.

Chloe was tired and drained of energy. She had no words to explain what she was feeling or going through, but she was sure of one thing. Her body, her mind, her spirit felt at peace. She recalled the Dark Man's voice but not his words. Because of that, she felt that it wasn't important to force her memory. For once in her life, she was at peace.

They all spent the next few days catching everyone up on the recent events, the new discoveries of the prophecy, the future, and what to do next. Chloe didn't seem troubled by the thought of the vampire Marcus. In fact, she forgot all about him. She did spend quite a bit of time alone in thought. The others worried about her, thinking she was depressed, when in reality, she was just getting to know her quiet spirit that lurked inside her. If Sarah Good needed to stay inside until later in Chloe's life when she could emerge, then she might as well try to make peace with her "new self."

CHAPTER TWELVE
BEGINNINGS

Summer finally came to an end and it was time to head back to Seattle. At first Chloe thought that it would just be her and her mom, but Tom surprised them by going back with them. The spirit of Sarah Good was at peace and only surfaced when Chloe drew on her powers. Their combined strength only gave Chloe courage and more recognition in the coven.

Sarah and Chloe managed to find the balance that they needed while Marlene kept studying the prophecy. Tom had always been her guide and that wouldn't stop. Chloe was finally happy, as she saw more and more visions of the future.

Chloe was a strong witch, even if she was only a teen. But her future looked bright and hopeful as the coven began to follow her. She could never be the leader, but Marija enjoyed the fact that the others were having inspiration for the Blood Prophecy.

SNEAK PEEK AT
AMBER: BIRTH OF A QUEEN

CHAPTER ONE
THE BIRTH

Nikoli looked back at Miriam as she was going into labor, and his thoughts raced back in time to the day he met her and how they'd married quickly. It was hard to believe that it had been a year since that day. Tuning out the sounds of her cries, he recalled how this beautiful woman wandered into his pack. It made him smile as he remembered.

There he and Shula were, gathering water and working the land as they were a nomadic pack, even for the 1980s in Delaware. As Nikoli came closer to the pond, he saw the foot hidden in the weeds. The pond was dense with weeds and made such a perfect hiding place. He looked at the foot and let his eyes move up farther. In his mind, he was hoping that this was not the remains of a human one of the pack

95

had decided to devour. His eyes continued to search and eventually Nikoli found a beautiful face. Around her neck was a green crystal amulet. The woman was beautiful and naked. Her face had a gash on her cheek and blood trickled from the side of her head.

Nikoli could see her chest rise and fall, though faintly. There was not much life in the woman. He bent down and picked her up. He didn't look at her curves or nakedness, but he moved fast to bring her back to the pack. Once she was healed, they spent a lot of time together, to the point where they began to develop feelings for each other. Nikoli, very old fashioned for a werewolf, loved her and wanted not only to consummate their relationship, but to begin a family together. He wanted her for his mate. Miriam agreed to his offer and they were wed. But after the wedding, Nikoli realized that he didn't know about her heritage, and that could pose an issue with the elders.

He asked Miriam to tell him of her family, and what she told him surprised him and left them with a lot of questions. He listened as Miriam told him her story.

"My parents are not all human. They are like you and your pack, but not quite werewolves. My family is also...shall we say, special, but in a way that might change your mind about me – "

Before she could continue to say the words that he didn't want to hear, Nikoli kissed her and reassured her. He wanted her to be his. He chose her.

"My father is what you would call, a seer. A prophet. But as such, he has special abilities that others do not. He could see into the past lives of people, supernatural or not. He could also move things with his mind, among other things. He belonged to an order, but I don't recall what order. My mother is a strong witch. She comes from a line of witches, or wiccans, or whatever they are called. But, her line of power is not at all what we would call the White Light of Power. When my parents married and formed a union, they left their families and their power behind until I was born. My birth changed things for them, and their destinies pulled them apart. I don't remember them after I turned five. I was the firstborn of a generation and my parents hid me. Soon after I turned five, a man came for me. I didn't learn why until much later. But I'd inherited my mother's fire and ran away many years later. I've been on my own since. I've been attacked, beaten, raped, and violated by people that knew my parents, but I don't know them. In fact, you found me after I was left for dead.

Here's what I know about the Dark Light of Power from my mom. There is a man that the covens

97

call the Tall Dark Man, who comes to certain witches and makes them fall under his control. Once they do, he uses their power and gives them more so that they serve him. My mother served him before I was born. My father thinks I am the child of the Dark Man, but I inherited his abilities, so I can't be. But my mother told me, the day I turned five, that if I ever have my first girl child, the Dark Man would come to claim her power unless a love stronger than true will help her to rise. My father told me also that this child I would come to have would rise above all and would be the queen to save the races, but her choices must be true and worthy of her heart. It is part of a prophecy that is told from generation to generation. In fact, all the races know this prophecy. If she ever strayed from her destiny, all would be lost. When they abandoned me, as I call it, they gave me this amulet to pass down and told me that my child must learn strength, love, and be faithful to the Blood Prophecy. I have yet to discover what all that means.

While I lived with this Dark Man, I learned the ways of the dark light and could barely recall the white light. In my dreams, I would hear some songs, but when I woke, there was nothing to remember.

Nikoli, love, I don't mean to scare you, but this child…if she is the child my parents spoke of, what shall we do? I don't want to lose her, but she must *be raised with her truth. But this is my family. You are my family."*

From that day forward, Nikoli loved her for the truth and her spirit, as it never led him away from her. But at the current moment, her screams brought him back to the moment. The birth. Looking at Miriam, he saw that her hair was drenched in sweat and clinging to her face, and tears were rolling down her cheeks as she screamed and pushed. One of the midwives from the pack was holding her legs while another let her rest against her. Both women were gently encouraging her to push.

"Push, Miriam. Push. Only a few more pushes. Bring this child forth. The pack is ready to love her. Atta girl."

Nikoli's love for her consumed him as he encouraged her to keep pushing. He didn't want to lose his love or this child. Nikoli closed his eyes and prayed to the heavens that this childbirth would not take his love. When his opened once more, he could see that Miriam was tired, blood seeped through the linens, and her bedding needed changing, but she had the fight in her to birth this child. Another woman entered the area and brought more clean water.

Women were rushing about and whispering.

Finally, a woman placed a warm mug in his hands and the smell of coffee filled his nostrils. She urged him to take a seat in the corner while the others helped his wife.

Before You Go...

HELP AN AUTHOR

write a review

THANK YOU!

Share your voice and help guide other readers to these wonderful books. Even if it's only a line or two your reviews help readers discover the author's books so they can continue creating stories that you'll love. Login to your favorite retailer and leave a review. Thank you.

Now Available

About the Author

Having been born and raised in Hawaii, I loved telling stories ever since I was a child about vampires, werewolves, angels, demons, and witches. I was a little girl who loved scary stories, much to my mother's dismay. The scarier - the better. Hawaii was a perfect place for stories until I moved to Seattle. I decided to turn a love for the supernatural into writing stories to see if others would love them as much as I do. Currently, I live in Florida but since I'm a Seattle girl at heart, my stories take place in the Northwest. I continue to write supernatural stories of vampires, werewolves, witches, and more while enjoying the beaches and sunshine.